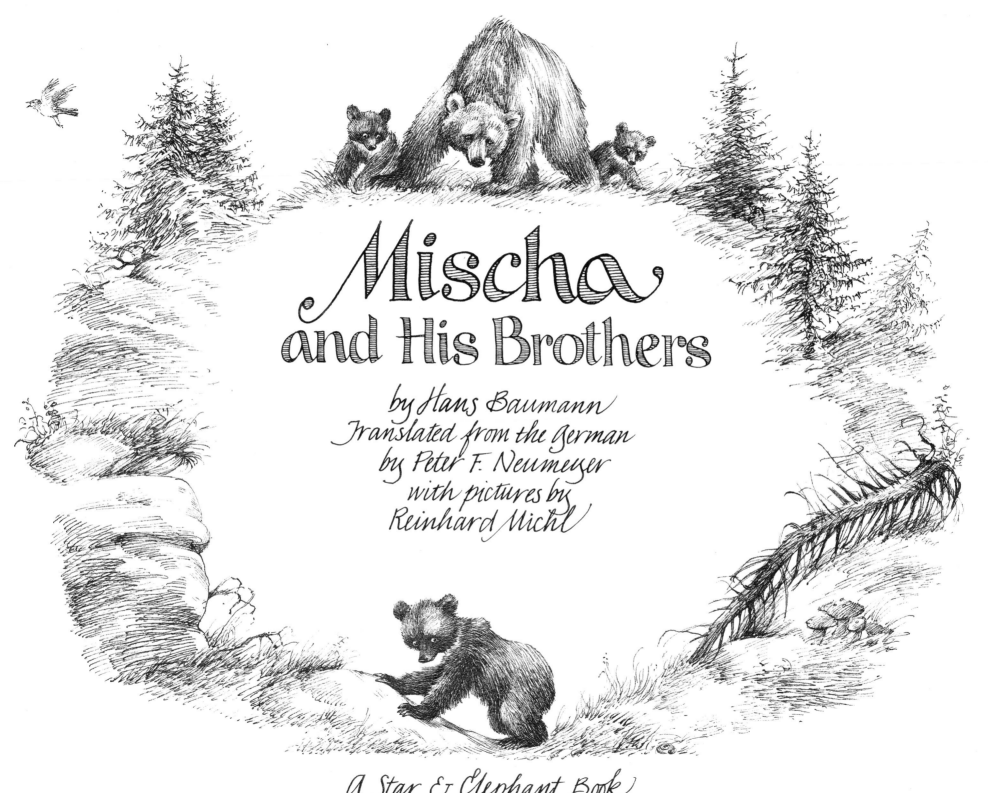

Mischa
and His Brothers

by Hans Baumann
Translated from the German
by Peter F. Neumeyer
with pictures by
Reinhard Michl

A Star & Elephant Book
The Green Tiger Press · La Jolla · California

It was on a day of many colors, an October day, that Mischa came home. The bears, his brothers, saw him coming from afar. It could only be he, since, except for him, no one else had been away. "It's him; he's coming back!"—that was the message all over the forest in which the bears lived. And all the bear brothers were beside themselves with happiness. During the three years that Mischa had been away, they did just what bears always do. In fat times, they had stuffed themselves so full that their hides could scarcely contain them and all their new flesh. And during the winter, snowed in up to their ears, they had slept. That was the life of a bear. They knew no other.

In the forest there was one bear who was so old that he had that light stripe around his neck that bears have either when they are very young or very old and wise. This old bear lived all alone in a cave. There the bear brothers sought him out when they were puzzled about something. He always gave good counsel. When Mischa was born, during the deep winter snow, the old bear had prophesied, "That one is going to have many adventures."

And the following fall, it began. One day Mischa disappeared from the forest. Of course at that time he wasn't called Mischa, since bears don't get names in the forest. The bear brothers hunted for him in all the thickets and in all the ravines. And then they gave up the search—and gave him up as well. None of the bear brothers gave any more thought to the young bear.

Then, one day, he returned to the forest. He was large and strong now, like his brothers. From a distance, he waved. And when he reached them, he kissed each in brotherly fashion.

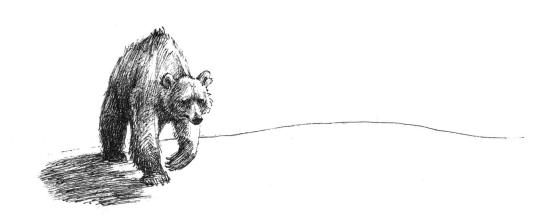

The bear brothers fell all over him with questions. "Tell us what it was like out there where none of us has ever been! We're your brothers, and we want to know." They all sat around him so not a word of his would escape them.

"I never did want to go away from you," the young bear began. "I ambled through the woods with nothing on my mind. It was a day just like today. The sun shone, and the whole forest was alive with colors. Suddenly I came to the path which led out of the forest.

"At the edge of the road sat a girl and an old man. The old man pulled something out of the leather bag which he had slung over his shoulder. He gave it to the girl. The wind wafted the scent that tickles bears' snouts. I was attracted to the two of them, and from closer up I saw a honeycomb which the girl held in her hand. The old man had one too. I sniffed the man. He smelled of bear. And I tell you, brothers, he smelled like us! So I went up to the two of them.

"'Go on, take it, Mischa, take it!' said the man, giving me a honeycomb. And so now my name was Mischa. I had a name—and I had a honeycomb. It tasted so good that honeycomb was all I could think of.

"The man said to the girl, 'Don't be afraid of Mischa!'

"But the girl was no longer in sight. She was under the coat the old man was wearing.

"'Come along with us, Mischa!' he said, and when I hesitated, he gave me a second honeycomb. All he had to do was to reach into the leather bag. I took the honeycomb, and when I had finished it, the forest was already far behind me.

"You may think the honey was to blame; or that I went along because the old man smelled of bear; or because I was so young and wanted to know what was out there in their world. But those reasons are merely part of the truth.

"You didn't see that girl. When I took the second comb, she pushed the coat aside and came forward and looked at me. She was still a little afraid. But when she saw I wouldn't hurt her, she began to smile. And then her own face became as bright as a honeycomb."

The bear brothers nodded. Their eyes sparkled at the thought of honey. Mischa saw this and he continued.

"The old man knew his way around bears. He also knew what bears were afraid of. When we came to a place where there was a humming of bees, he lit his pipe and blew little clouds of smoke out of it. Soon he was surrounded by a cloud. He went to the beehive—and returned—with honey. And he didn't have to run away from the bees. No bear can do such a thing!"

"And the girl?" the bear brothers asked.

"She was only a very little girl," said Mischa. "The first day she stayed on the right side of the old man, because I stayed on his left. When night came, a cold night, the old man said to the girl: 'It's good that Mischa came along—look at his fur! It will keep you warm.'

"And to me he said, 'You're not going to let the girl be cold, are you, Mischa?'

"I felt I was important, and kept the girl warm as well as I was able, all through the night. And when morning came and the old man asked, 'Well, how did you sleep?' the girl said, 'Like a cloud.'

" 'And warm too?'

" 'Like in an oven!'

"From that time on, the old man stayed on the right and I stayed on the left, and the girl walked in the middle."

"And you had honey every day?" asked one bear.

"Not every day," Mischa admitted, "but always without bee stings. Listen. As long as I went from place to place with those two, we had enough to eat. People in the cities and towns were happy when they saw us. Only the animals that lived in the towns acted dumb. The chickens cackled; the geese honked; the dogs barked as though we were a mob. And all because of me. But the children were our friends, and that was our blessing, for friends know right away when someone is hungry. Even the grownups came over to us because the girl did something that made everybody happy."

The bear brothers looked up. "And what did the girl do?"

"The girl danced," said Mischa. "She twirled as effortlessly as a leaf in the wind. The old man drummed on his small drum, and in between he blew on a willow flute. The people clapped. Then the old man turned the drum upside down and passed back and forth among the people. They threw money into that drum. But it was the children who brought us food. One day the old man nudged me and said, 'If only you could dance, Mischa—just think how much more the children would bring us!'

"So I tried. It wasn't easy. But the old man had lots of patience. He and the girl showed me everything, and in the end he wasn't all that sure who danced better—the girl or I. I danced like a bear; the girl like a girl—but it was just this that must have pleased the people most. And always when I danced, I held a rose. And when the dancing was over, I gave it to the girl. And then the people just didn't want to stop clapping. And, in truth, the old man was right. They threw many more coins into the drum now."

"Dance for us," the bears called excitedly.

At first Mischa didn't want to.

"It's not something you can do here in the forest. And there aren't any people to watch."

The bears clamored, "Aren't we *anyone*?"

"The girl ought to be here," said Mischa.

And then a bear tore up a little tree, bit off the roots, and stuck the tree into the ground in front of Mischa.

"There, you've got your girl!"

Mischa broke off a branch with red leaves and began to dance. One could hear a bird, and Mischa recalled the willow flute and turned about. Now he was larger than the bear brothers. They looked up to him, and they were pleased. They even hummed along. At the end, they had so much fun that they too wanted to dance. "Come on, show us," they begged Mischa.

Mischa resisted. They, however, wouldn't let him alone until he showed them just the way that he himself had started. He danced a few easy steps and turned on his hind legs. The brothers imitated him—that is to say, they tried. But they fell down like overstuffed sacks. First they thought it amusing when one fell down, and all the others laughed at him. Then each one of them noticed that he, too, fell down, and that the others would joke about *him*. So then the game wasn't so much fun anymore. "How in the world can a bear devote himself to dancing!" one called out. "And for three years, at that!"

They backed away from Mischa and looked at him with puzzlement, through different eyes. Mischa was frightened.

"What's wrong with you?" he asked. "I'm not going to do this anymore; it's all over with."

"You *did* do it," said one of the bears.

"A bear who has any self-respect doesn't do such a thing."

"I was hungry," Mischa said. "And after all, I couldn't let the girl be cold."

"And you had to give her the red rose!" another mocked so that the others laughed.

Now for the first time Mischa noticed that he was still holding onto the branch with the red leaves. He let it drop. The bird no longer sang. The bear brothers squatted there like boulders. None of them looked at him.

Then Mischa said, "It wasn't easy for me out there. Often my feet burned as though I'd been walking through fire. On black roads, cars drove louder and faster than the wind. And there are streets that are made of iron. And trains roll on them, dark as

thunderclouds. We went from one country to another in the night, when it rained so hard that our tracks were washed away. For that's the way it is among people. Even though they're all people, they have different countries, and for everyone there is but one land, his own. The old man and the girl, however, didn't belong anywhere. In the winter, it was especially hard for us. The old man and the girl couldn't let themselves be snowed in, the way we bears do. When the hunger raged, the old man went into towns and came back with chickens. And if the girl

asked, 'Where are these from?' then he said, 'From nowhere—just like ourselves.'

"And those chickens from nowhere tasted better than any others, I can tell you! Well, brothers, what do you think we looked like when spring began to arrive? We had to be careful not to be blown away by the wind, we were so thin. On such days, I thought about you and about the forest."

"And why didn't you come back?" a bear asked.

"But I did come back," Mischa said.

"Why not earlier?"

"You wouldn't believe how cold a little girl can get," Mischa said. "There were winter nights when our breath was taken away. The stars sparkled like frozen lightning. We crawled into sheds. I had to make the girl warm so she wouldn't freeze. I couldn't leave in the winter."

"But why not in the summer?"

"Because that's when the old man was piping. And drumming. That was dancing time. Believe me, I didn't want to go on, but I couldn't get away from him."

"And why not?"

"Because I was attached to him. By a chain. So—now you know."

The bear brothers stared at him as though they had never seen him before. One asked him sharply, "How could you let it get to that point?"

"The old man had more than honeycombs in his leather bag," Mischa said. "More than the drum and the willow flute—it was a bag with a lot in it. A chain too. And one day he took it out. The day had begun better than many other days. The girl and I danced, and no chicken owners were watching, only wanderers like us. They had colorful wagons, and we got enough to eat. The wanderers kept small fires burning. They were blacksmiths. They made all sorts of things, including rings. One of them gave the girl a silver ring.

"I got a ring too. It was made of iron. I watched as it was being made; I was curious. Suddenly I was grabbed. And one of them shoved a horrible pair of pliers into my nose. When I came to, I was attached to a chain. I tore at it and roared. The old man offered me a honeycomb. 'It has to be, Mischa. A bear as big as you are can't go among people if he isn't on a chain.'

"I didn't eat anything for three days. The old man wore a wide belt. He fastened the chain to it. From that day on, I was attached to him, and couldn't get away anymore. If I didn't want to dance, he pulled at the chain."

"But you're here," exclaimed one. "Where is the chain?"

Mischa's eyes sparked. "The old man had me dance now whenever it suited him. He couldn't get enough. Once, when people had given him drink, he boasted of me: 'My Mischa dances as long as I want him to. If I want him to, he'll dance the whole night through.'

No one believed him. So the old man made a bargain with the farmer: 'If Mischa stops dancing before the sun comes up, you get to keep him—and what do you bet against that?'

" 'Ten chickens.'

" 'Too few. I want a hundred.'

" 'Good, a hundred chickens,' the farmer shouted.

"The old man let me dance. Sometimes he drummed and sometimes he piped. And every once in a while he tugged at the chain.

" 'Just keep dancing along,' he called, as he noticed that I was becoming enraged. The girl wasn't there. She was sleeping in a shed that belonged to the host.

The old man made me dance because he wanted a hundred chickens. When he tugged at the chain, I saw a red spot in front of my eyes. The red spot got bigger. And suddenly there was a red sun in front of me. I saw it rise. Then I took a leap and ripped myself loose. I heard the chain strike the ground. The old man bellowed. But nothing could hold me back now. The red sun danced in front of my eyes. When I had run for an hour, the red sun disappeared. I saw that it was still night, and ran further. Finally the real sun that rises every day rose in the very direction I was running. Just think, brothers, the sun had come out of our own forest. Now you know everything."

The bear brothers looked past him as though they were searching for something. One of them said, "You are no longer the way you used to be."

"Naturally," said Mischa. "I'm a full grown bear now—just like you."

The bear brothers shook their heads. "You can never again be like us."

"Why not?" asked Mischa.

"You're still chained to *him*," declared the bear.

And then Mischa became angry. "Just let that old man come this way now. I'd show him what a bear is!"

"I don't mean chained to the old man," said the bear brother. "I mean to the girl."

Then Mischa looked at the little tree that stood before him. And then he said, "It's just as you say. I *am* attached to the girl. If it had been only the little girl, and not the old man too—I'd never have come back to you."

"There, that's just it!" shouted the bear brothers.

Mischa said, "You don't understand me. When I thought about the chain, I was glad that I had run away; as soon as I thought of the girl, I was drawn back."

"Well then, go," said the bear who had fallen down more often than the others when he tried to dance.

"You're a dancing bear, and you always will be."

"And you've got a name," one declared.

"We don't."

"But the worst thing is—you were on the chain," shouted a third bear.

"I'm no longer on one," said Mischa.

"What you once were, you will always be," the bear brothers reproached him.

Mischa looked up at the bear brothers quizzically. And now the bear brothers noticed.

"You bear the mark!" one shouted. "You can see it on your nose, that you were on a chain!"

Then Mischa roared, "You can still see it *because* I tore myself loose!"

"And will one always be able to see it just that way?" they asked him.

Mischa didn't answer them anymore. He left. Only one young bear looked after him. "We shouldn't have let him go," he said.

"Why not?" the others persisted. "He made us all look ridiculous."

The bear brothers argued for a long time. Then one suggested: "Let's go to the old bear. He's what a bear ought to be. He can tell us whether it was right to let him run off."

So they went off to the old bear. The old bear sat in front of the cave, in the sun. From far off, the bear brothers saw the light stripe around his neck. When they reached him, they recounted what had happened. The old bear listened patiently. Finally they said, "You're the bear who gives wise counsel. Tell us, was it right that we let him run off?"

"It doesn't matter in the slightest what you do with him," said the old bear. "He is attached to you, whether you look for him or not."

"Won't he disappear from the forest again?"

"No," the old bear assured them. "Now he will remain here."

"But what will he do?"

"He'll find himself a cave, and if someone is looking for him, that's where he can be found," said the old bear. "And everyone will say that that's a bear like a bear ought to be; that he is a bear who will always give good counsel. Why? Because he has been beyond the forest. Because he has been around. And because he was on a chain and tore himself away. Small wonder that someone like him knows about all sorts of things that didn't grow in the forest. Naturally it will take time until others are aware of it. It has taken time with me too."

"But you haven't been on a chain!" protested a bear brother.

The old bear then lifted his head aslant and blinked into the sun. And all the bears saw where the ring had been.

Now none of them asked anything further. The old one, however, bent down slightly and said, "One thing I'd still like to know—what his name is. For, after all, he has got a name."

"Mischa," one said.

"Great Sun in the Heavens!" exclaimed the old bear. "Even that, too!"

And he beamed.

HANS BAUMANN
was born in Amberg on April 22,
1914. He taught in a one-room
schoolhouse in the Bavarian woods
in 1933–34. Early in his career, he
wrote songs and plays, and after the
war years, which he spent in Russia
and in internment in France, he
devoted himself to writing books
for children and young people. His
books have been translated into
23 languages, and he has translated
numerous children's books from the
Russian. Hans Baumann has lived in
Murnau for the past thirty years.

REINHARD MICHL
was born in Lower Bavaria in 1948.
He completed professional training
as a typesetter, and studied graphic
design. He also studied painting at
the Academy of Formal Arts in
Munich, where he lives today as
a freelance illustrator. His first
American publication was
*Mr. Death and the Red-headed
Woman* by Helen Eustis, a Star &
Elephant Book from The Green
Tiger Press.

Copyright © 1984 by K. Thienemanns Verlag, Stuttgart. All rights reserved.
English translation copyright © 1985 by The Green Tiger Press, La Jolla, California.
This edition published by The Green Tiger Press for sale in the United States and Canada only.
Manufactured in the Federal Republic of Germany.
ISBN: 0-88138-051-2
Library of Congress Catalog Card Number: 85-070603
First Edition • First Printing

The text was set in Garamond by Professional Typography, San Diego, California.
Color separation by Frank Kreyssig, Germering, F.R.G.
Printed by Hablitzel + Sohn, Dachau. Bound by Sigloch, Künzelsau.